	DATE DUE		

The Conspiracy of the Secret Nine

By Celia Bland

Illustrated by
Donald L. Williams

SILVER MOON PRESS
NEW YORK

First Silver Moon Press Edition 1995

Copyright © 1995 by Celia Bland
Illustration copyright © 1995 by Donald L. Williams

For information write:

Silver Moon Press
126 Fifth Avenue
Suite 803
New York, NY 10011
(800) 874-3320

Project Editor & Designer: Eliza Booth

Library of Congress Cataloging-in-Publication Data

Bland, Celia
The Conspiracy of the Secret Nine / by Celia Bland;
illustrated by Donald L. Williams.—1st Silver Moon Press ed.
p.   cm. — (Mysteries in time)
Summary: In 1898 in Wilmington, N.C., on the verge of elections
that will determine the course of local segregation and the
fate of black residents, Troy and Randy encounter a mystery
that could tear the city apart.
ISBN 1-881889-67-X ($12.95)
[Race relations–Fiction. 2. Afro-Americans–Fiction. 3. Wilmington
(N.C.)–History–Fiction. 4. Mystery and detective stories.] I. Williams,
Donald L., ill. II. Title. III. Series.
Pz7.B599Co   1995
[Fic]–dc20   95-8573
                                   CIP
                                         AC

10 9 8 7 6 5 4 3 2 1

Printed in the USA

TABLE OF CONTENTS

FOREWORD

The Conspiracy of the Secret Nine takes place in Wilmington, North Carolina, some thirty years after the Civil War. A mecca for ambitious African-Americans, by 1890, sixty percent of Wilmington's population was black. The city boasted one of the few African-American daily newspapers in the U.S., and many elected and appointed government officials were African-Americans.

At the time the story begins, Wilmington was controlled by an elected government of liberal Republicans, many of them either black or transplanted northerners. The governor himself, a native of Wilmington, did much to insure that desegregation was furthered at every level of government and commerce.

Wilmington was also the home of a determined group of segregationists known as the White Government Union. These men, commonly called the Redeemers, wanted to ban African-Americans from government, deny them the right to vote, close the black schools, and stop the integration of white neighborhoods. They knew they could not reinstate slavery as an institution, but they hoped to render southern blacks powerless by robbing them of their rights and their livelihoods.

In November, 1898, on the eve of city elections, Republicans and Democrats were gearing up for battle. The prize would be absolute control of Wilmington's future as a segregated or desegregated city. The consequences of this election would affect the whole nation.

THE HIDING
PLACE

"**T**ROY! TROY! WHERE ARE YOU HIDING?"

It was Momma and I could tell by the way she hollered my name that she was angry. Laying my cheek against the rough bark of the tree limb where I was perched, I held my breath and hoped I'd be lost among the leaves. From here, the big oak tree in my best friend's yard, I could hear everything going on at my house without being seen.

Suddenly, the branch jounced, and a head of bright red hair popped up through the leaves. A hoarse whisper: "What are you doing in my tree, boy?"

"You hush up, boy," I retorted.

Randy Hollis shimmied up the trunk and straddled my branch.

"Your momma's hunting you," he said sternly. "You haven't killed any cats, have you?"

"No," I said. "That Callie was pestering me, so I hung her rag doll from the bedpost." Callie is my little sister, eight years old and one hundred percent vexation.

"I guess we should plan the funeral," Randy laughed, waggling his red eyebrows comically. "Will you be bringing some cold meats to the wake, Brother Troy?"

A guffaw burst from my throat and I clapped both hands over my mouth.

"If anybody needs burying, it's that Rory," he continued. "I tell you what, we were digging clams this morning and he—"

"Digging?" I hissed. "I thought you and I were going together!"

"Well, I can't be waiting for you all the time. Now you're working with your poppa at the barbershop, I never see you, unless you're hiding out in my tree."

"But listen," he added, leaning forward, "tonight's the full moon and—"

From the foot of the tree there came a bull–like bellow: "Son, are you up in that tree?"

Randy went pale beneath his freckles. "Yes, Poppa," he quavered. He swung down from the limb swift as a peddler's monkey. "Here I am."

"Troy Worth, are you up there, too?" Mr. Hollis yelled.

"Yes, sir," I muttered. Slowly, slowly, my heart in my mouth, I began climbing down. Mr. Hollis had anchored himself at the roots of the tree and he pushed his face right into mine as I slid down the trunk. He was balling his hands into fists as if he couldn't wait to give me a clout. I looked over the top of his porkpie hat into Randy's unhappy face. There was real fear in Randy's eyes.

Jumping the last few feet to the ground, I moved crabways toward my yard. Momma was standing on our front porch, glaring at me.

Mr. Hollis kept his mud-colored eyes on my face. He rested his hands on his hips and swaggered over into our yard, just as if it belonged to him.

"Haven't I told you to keep your boy out of my oak tree?" he bawled. "If I find him there one more time, girl, I start shooting."

Momma's hand crawled up the front of her dress to her throat. "Troy," she said, her voice low but steady, "get yourself inside the house right this minute."

I kept my eyes on my feet as I jogged to our front porch. I was careful to stay out of the reach of Mr. Hollis's fists. From the corner of my eye, I saw him give Randy a shove between the shoulder–blades.

"You keep away from that negrah," he said loudly.

My mother took my ear between her forefinger and thumb and hustled me up the porch steps. "You just wait until your daddy gets home," she muttered, as the screen door slammed behind us.

IT WAS SUPPERTIME BEFORE DADDY SAID ONE WORD TO me. All during the meal Momma acted as though I'd done something so horrible that it showed on my face

3

like a scar. I pushed the cornbread and white beans around on my plate, my stomach in knots. Even Callie avoided my glance. I could tell she was trying not to look too pleased that I was going to catch it.

Finally, Daddy put down his fork and knife. He sighed.

"That was delicious, Adelle," he said. He looked off into space a minute before pushing back his chair.

"Troy, I want to see you out on the back porch."

I rose reluctantly and followed him outside. The back porch was where Daddy offered up punishment. Tonight he didn't take the strop down from its hook. When I risked a glance at his face, it was more weary and sad than wrathful.

"Troy," he said, as he lowered himself down to the porch step. "I hear you got into a scrape today."

"Yes, sir," I muttered. "That Callie—"

"No," he interrupted me, "I'm not talking about the devilment you get up to with your sister— though let me tell you that a boy almost twelve years old is too big for such foolishness. Callie's going to need your protection one day, and woe to you if you aren't around."

I nodded as though I understood. But I didn't.

"No," he said, "I'm talking about something else. You disobeyed your mother and you disobeyed me when you hid in Mr. Hollis's tree. We've both told you not to go over there. That man doesn't have a job. He just lies around and drinks. Now, I know you boys are friends. That's something that worries your momma

4

and myself. But your momma was mighty fond of Mrs. Hollis, and so we're willing to let you both pal around so long as it's not on Mr. Hollis's property."

Both of us looked over into the Hollis's back-yard. Our land is staked out with Momma's tomato plants and snap beans. Along the edge, to keep bugs away, she's put in some sharp-smelling marigolds. But where the flowers stop, the Hollis's yard begins. Nothing grows, not even grass. There's just a circle of hard-packed dirt and an iron stake where Mr. Hollis's old hunting dog used to pace around and around at the length of his chain. That dog died last spring around the time cholera carried off Mrs. Hollis.

Daddy sighed. "Troy, we're living at the best possible time for black people," he said. "This city is thriving, and it's our labor that's making it grow. You know I own the barbershop free and clear—"

I nodded.

"And you know that most of my customers are white. Do you know how rare that is in the South? I'm proud to live in a city where I can rub elbows with black men like Lawyer Armand Upton and B. Sullivan Leigh. They're educated, wealthy, and mix with senators and other white folks as equals. And they are!" he said. He slapped his open hand onto his knee.

"They are equal, and we are, too, Troy. Don't ever forget that. President Lincoln declared our free-dom, and the War Between the States guaranteed equality. For two hundred and fifty years our people were slaves—" He stopped.

Daddy and Momma had both been born slaves down in rice country. They never talked about it, but Momma sometimes woke us up in the middle of the night, screaming from a nightmare.

My father shook himself out of his reverie. He took my chin between his big forefinger and thumb and turned me around to face him.

"Troy, it's 1898, and we're free to live however we please. Take a look at our neighborhood! Colored and white families side by side. But not all white people are happy about that. Some want us to be slaves again so that they'll have somebody to look down on."

"But Dad," I said, "if Randy and I are equals, how come Mr. Hollis doesn't want us to play together?"

"Son, it seems to me that when a man has lost his wife and his livelihood, he often tries to find somebody to blame it on. Mr. Hollis has decided that black folks are responsible for his bad luck. You hanging from that man's tree just gives him an excuse to try and hurt us. I don't want unpleasantness where I live. So I'm telling you now, and I mean it: Stay out of the Hollis's yard."

"Yes, sir," I mumbled.

"Good. Now go to bed. If I hear one more complaint from your momma this week, I'll give you a hiding you won't soon forget." He reached out to swat the back of my head.

"Yes, Daddy," I said, ducking.

"You getting too fast for me, son." He laughed.

CALLIE BREATHED EVENLY BESIDE ME. I STARED UP INTO the dark and mulled over Daddy's words. The thing that confused me the most was how my family could be equal to the Hollises when my momma allowed Mr. Hollis to call her "girl" as though she was his servant. Somehow I knew she hadn't told my daddy about that.

THE RING
OF FIRE

A GOOD BOY WOULD HAVE ROLLED OVER AND GONE BACK TO
sleep when he heard a knocking on the window
pane. But I never did what was good for me. I'd been
expecting that knock. I had what Lawyer Upton might
call a prior engagement.

Slowly and carefully so as not to wake Callie, I
slipped out of the bed and peeked outside. There was
Randy, his face pressed horribly against the window,
grinning like a jack-o'lantern.

"Blackbeard's treasure," he mouthed. He jerked
his head toward the street.

It was just about midnight. The moon was full and
shining like blazes, exactly the right time to go along to
Burnt Mill Creek. Randy believed Blackbeard the pirate
had buried his treasure at the creek. He'd got a hair ball
from a grizzled old sailor down at the docks.

"It'll find anything you set it on," the old salt had sworn. "Just put it on a tree trunk under the light of the full moon and say the magic spell."

The spell was a secret. Sailor Pete had whispered it to Randy, and Randy wouldn't tell it even to me. Still, he'd offered to let me help dig up the treasure. And half the treasure was to be mine!

The porch screen squeaked once, loudly, and I stood stock still for what seemed hours, waiting. Nothing moved and nobody called out, so I went on down the steps and reached underneath the porch for the pickax and the shovel I'd stashed there.

Randy had moved into the street. Without saying a word, I handed him the shovel, and we took off down Bladen Avenue. There are no gas lamps in our neck of the woods, but the moon was almost bright as the sun. I wasn't scared. I had the pickax over my shoulder.

"Randy, what do you expect Blackbeard buried in that treasure chest?"

"Jewels," said Randy. "Rubies and diamonds and black pearls and doubloons. That's what all the pirates collected, and Blackbeard was the biggest and meanest pirate of them all."

"How did the navy come to catch him then?"

"A Virginia navy captain helped bushwhack Blackbeard just as he was slipping back from burying his treasure. Eagle's Island is where they nabbed him. Tortured him, too, trying to find out where the riches were. Old Blackbeard, he was so mean, he wouldn't say a word. So they cut off his head and left it to rot on a pole down by the docks. The whole town came gaping around, but the smell of it soon drove 'em back."

Randy paused for breath. He's Irish, and my daddy says the Irish are talkers.

"Everybody figured that Blackbeard's treasure was buried on Eagle Island, where he could get to it easily from his ship. That's foolishness. Anybody would think of that. Naw, he buried it out at Burnt Mill Creek, where nobody goes. That's what Sailor Pete told me, and he should know. Why, his poppa sailed with Blackbeard!"

I digested this news. "Then how come Sailor Pete hasn't dug up the treasure?"

"Because, silly, he's afraid of Blackbeard's ghost! It lies there, waiting for somebody to come, and then it jumps on their back and sucks their soul right out of their ears!"

Chills ran up and down my backbone. "What's to stop Blackbeard from doing that to us?"

"The hair ball will protect us, bonehead. Besides, we've never killed anybody like Sailor Pete has. Ghosts can't hurt us."

I wasn't convinced, but I didn't let on. We took a left on Miller Street. There was nobody about, just a calico cat edging along an iron gate.

Randy reached down for a stone. He sidearmed it at the cat, but he missed, and the stone sounded a racket against the fence.

"Shh, you fool," I hissed.

Randy narrowed his eyes. "That's old man

Heeks's gate, isn't it, boy? Isn't he the man your ma works for?"

"Yeah," I said warily. Sam Heeks owns a pawn shop in town that caters to the sailors and bargemen who blow in, ready for a good time. Mr. Heeks also lends money and sells property. Some say he's the richest white man in town, but that doesn't make him loved. Too many people in Wilmington owe him money. But my momma is Mr. Heeks's cook, and she doesn't say nothing against him.

"Isn't his wife about the color of that iron gate?" Randy sneered.

"Mebbe," I said. "What business is it of yours?"

"You'd think your momma would want to work for respectable folks," he retorted, and he winked one green eye.

I made the mistake of coming at him with my left fist rather than my right. He saw it and ducked, but I slipped my leg behind his knees and pushed him while he was still off balance. Then, we were down in the dust.

"Eat dirt!" I yelled, but Randy pulled his legs up under him and flipped me over his head. We had both gotten to our feet and were ready to battle again, when a flicker of something fiery made us stop and look around.

"What's that?" Randy gasped. He was breathing hard.

The street was dead quiet except for a whisper of wind, and then we heard a murmur, a melancholy sound off in the distance.

11

"Blackbeard himself!" I whispered. I didn't say it too loud for fear that Randy would call me lily-livered.

"Let's go see," he said. I followed him into the shade of the elms lining Mill Street and onto the cross-road. The wind picked up with a whoosh, and the trees tossed their branches up and back.

"There's somebody in the burying ground," Randy breathed, his voice quivering with excitement. He was like a bird dog, all his strength gathered up in his neck and shoulders. He pointed to an archway made of blocks of granite; cut in the granite were big curlicue letters that spelled Fairmont.

Beyond, down the curving gravel path, I saw a wavering circle of fire.

"It's ghosts!" I hissed. "Let's get out of here!"

"That isn't no ghost," Randy scoffed. "Since when do ghosts carry torches?"

He was right. The wind carried the stink of sulfur and paraffin.

"Randy Hollis," I retorted, "don't you never read the Bible? That's fire and brimstone! It's the Devil himself!"

That stopped him in his tracks. He grabbed hold of my arm and whispered excitedly into my ear.

"Naw, it's not the Devil, Troy, it's the Ghost Soldier! I heard he appeared today at the livery stable and asked for water for his bony mare. Burwell Poteat brought four buckets before the nag finished drinking. Then the soldier said, 'Thank ye. My horse ain't had a drink since we lost Fort Fisher,'—and poof! he just plain disappeared."

That was enough for me. The Ghost Soldier was always seen around Wilmington at election time, getting white people riled up about losing Fort Fisher during the war and the city being taken by the Yankee soldiers. I'd heard Momma tell Daddy that where the Ghost Soldier leads, the Ku Klux Klan is soon to follow.

I reached out for Randy's elbow and tried to pull him back. He wrenched free and slipped under the archway without a word. I stood in the darkness of the street, alone. Whether this was the Devil, or ghosts, or the Ku Kluxers, it wasn't anything I wanted to get mixed up in.

I dug my toe into the dust. I couldn't go home! Not and face Randy tomorrow, crowing over me, calling me yellow–bellied before all the boys. I sighed. Then I strolled into the cemetery.

Under my hand the granite arch was cold as a well digger's wallet. I could make out a little hill in front of me, a statue at its top. On both sides of the path were sweet-smelling bushes and the craziest looking gravestones. One was fashioned into a tree trunk split by an axe. Another was a marble urn wrapped in a marble blanket. I knew for sure that none of my people were buried here. We laid our folks to rest under a blanket of sand that the women traced with cunning patterns.

I looked around for Randy. He'd taken cover in back of a headstone so large that it must have named a whole family. I bent double and tiptoed to his side. He nearly jumped free of his skin when I touched my

13

hand to his cheek. That gave me a certain satisfaction.

"Close your eyes," he muttered crossly. "They glow like a hell hound's."

I stood still beside him and turned my glowing eyes toward the statue on the hill. It was of a soldier in a greatcoat resting his rifle, butt down, between his feet. The ring of fire was just beneath it.

"What's going on, Randy?" I whispered.

"I don't know."

"Who's that statue?"

Randy turned his head and gave me a look of contempt. "That's the Confederate War Memorial," he whispered. "Now, run!"

Then he took off up the hill. I swallowed hard and dashed after him. We came to rest behind a crepe myrtle bush, about ten feet below the circle. I could clearly see that the ghosts were men. Some of them were dressed in work clothes, others wore long white gowns with peaked hoods. A few carried guns. The leader stood ramrod-straight, like a preacher or a soldier. He was short-statured and had a white handlebar mustache and a tiny pointed beard.

My heart was pounding in my ears. It was a full five minutes before I could hear what the preacher was saying.

"They were men," he proclaimed. His eyes glittered in the torchlight. "White men who faced the dangers of the battlefield, the fatigues of long marches, the hunger, and the bloody battles of Bull Run and Little Round Top. White men who died for the ideals of the white race. Brothers, will we betray those men?"

"No! No!" his listeners rumbled. The torches flared. I shut my eyes, sick with dread. Were these the Ku Klux Klan after all?

"In two days," the man said, "Wilmington holds her elections. There's a conspiracy afoot to keep the Republicans who run our schools, our police force, our waterfront, in office. The uppity black lawyers who defend the multitudes of black criminals; the Republican carpetbaggers who make money hand over fist while we starve; the shiftless layabouts who lounge in the shade of the juniper tree while we sweat under the hot sun; these are the conspirators against the white race! These are the Republicans we must grind into the dust!"

"Our city is unsafe for our women and children. Why, Wilmington is known from Atlanta to Richmond as the capital of crime! Just last week a lowly black woman took her umbrella and prodded the wife of a leading Democrat off the sidewalk and into the street! Was justice served? Not, by God, by the Republican judge. No, that sassy black lawyer started in, and the jury virtually rewarded the miscreant for her assault. We here tonight are an independent Democratic jury. We found her guilty and we levied punishment—didn't we boys? She'll wear the mark of our wrath until Judgement Day!"

The crowd roared. When the speaker stepped from the shadow of the statue into the torchlight, I nearly jumped out my skin, his expression was that hateful.

"White brothers," he shouted, "take back your birthright! When the Southern War of Independence was lost, I and my company were left stranded in the hostile land of Pennsylvania. I walked all the way back to Wilmington. It took me two months. When I reached my home soil, I fell down and kissed the earth. That's how much I love this city. Thousands of our brothers in arms did not survive that sacred conflict. Some lie buried here beneath our feet. They will not be forgotten. The Cape Fear River will run bloody red before we surrender our fair city to a ragged rabble of Republicans!"

The men let out a cheer. My knees gave out, and I sank down behind the bush, choking on the stink of its flowers.

Randy was perfectly still. It dawned on me that he was staring at one man in particular who had stepped into the light to pump the speaker's hand. Something about the man's profile. Something about the way his hat was pulled down over his eyes.

"Randy!" The word burst out of me in a horrified bleat. "There's your daddy!"

Randy turned to look at me. His face, reddened in the reflected light of the torches, was like one of the evil-featured masks the sailors sell down by the docks. I must have pulled away from him, because the next thing I knew I was on my back in the dewy grass and Randy was gone, a blur of bare feet leaping over the well-tended graves.

THE GOLDEN
AGE

"TROY, YOU'D BETTER GET UP OR MOMMA WILL TAN YOUR HIDE."
I curled myself deeper into the bedclothes. Callie jerked the pillow from under my head and whacked me with it.

"Hurry up, Troy. The grits are getting cold."

She stomped off. I was left alone to contemplate the morning light yellowing the wooden walls. I felt a great weight on my chest, pressing me into the bed. My eyes felt like sinkers.

Momma was serving breakfast when I stumbled into the kitchen. She reached down the earthenware jar from the shelf beside the stove and dribbled a little molasses into my bowl of hominy grits.

"Eat, boy. You know I've got to get to work," she scolded. She bent down to retrieve a pan of warmed-over cornbread from the oven.

"Here your Daddy goes and hires you to work for him, and you're already late."

I groaned. I'd only been working at the barbershop since last week, and this morning the job had slipped my mind. Before, I had only to manage Callie while Momma and Daddy worked, and I could take my time waking up. Most of the time I was messing around in the yard with Randy, anyway, and Callie was watching herself. But ever since Mr. Hollis had lost his job as a ship's carpenter, and started sitting on his porch all day, drinking whiskey and cursing, Momma had been worried. Finally, Daddy had decided that Callie would stay with Junie Bates's momma, and I should come help him.

Chewing slowly, I watched Momma fold her apron into her string bag. She straightened her hat at the little mirror above the sink.

"Callie, you walk over to the Bates's with Troy," she said. "I'll comb out your hair tonight. Troy," she added, with a glance at me, "get a move on."

She kissed us both on the cheek and set off to cook fine white grits and fluffy biscuits for the Heeks's breakfast.

BY THE TIME I DRAGGED MYSELF DOWN OUR FRONT STEPS, the streets were bustling. Carts rumbled to and fro, freighted with turnips, beets, and sweet potatoes for shipment on the Carolina Central Railway, or with salted fish, barrels of sugar and salt, and jugs of rum for the big farms outside town. The farmers sat up high on their buckboards, smiling genially at passersby.

When a rice planter trotted past in a dusty old buggy, the farmers lifted their straw hats. The rice planters' families had owned slaves before the war, and some of them had even fought in it. But rice planting, Daddy said, was a bad crop nowadays. Only the poorest black folks would work up to their ankles in water, planting and harvesting the rice, no matter how much planters paid them—and the pay was never much.

"Too poor to paint, too proud to whitewash" people said about the old Wilmington families that had fallen on hard times. They were just as proud wearing calico as they had been wearing fine silks. A rice planter might lift one finger from the reins when greeting a cabbage farmer, but he wouldn't tip his hat, no matter how well off that farmer was.

"Where did you go last night, Troy?"

Callie's quizzing voice pulled me out of my musings.

"What do you mean, girl?"

"Don't lie, Troy. I heard you coming in this morning. Daddy's going to tan your hide when he finds out."

"Oh-ho! So you going to carry tales? Well, just wait and see what happens to poor Euphonia!"

"Don't you hurt my doll, Troy! I'll tell on you for sure!"

"Okay, Miss Priss, I won't hurt your silly doll. I went to see a man about a horse. That's all."

Callie stopped in the street. "Did Randy go with you?"

"Mebbe," I said, and kept walking.

"He isn't your friend anymore, Troy," she called after me.

I turned back to look at her. She was still my little sister, wearing a checked dress a little tight under the arms and scuffed lace-ups, but her round face was solemn. The expression in her eyes reminded me of Momma's, deep and sad.

"What'd you say?"

Without another word, she dashed past me down the street and vanished through the Bates's front gate.

In spite of the fine October sunshine, I felt a chill in my bones. When Mrs. Etheridge, her arms filled with fresh flowers to sell at the market, yelled out a "How-do," I only nodded. Stopping at the pump for a drink, I spotted Big Isaac Samuels, the overseer at the cotton compress. He stood at attention and saluted me as though I was a ship's captain. That made me feel better. I stood up straight and saluted back smartly.

The closer to the river I got, the more banks and offices and shops I passed. At Fifth Avenue the boardwalks began, and the gas lamps. Now the streets were filled with white women doing their shopping. Like tugboats, they had servants in their wake, loaded with straw baskets and string bags.

"Hey-O! Fish I got 'em! I got butterbeans! I got corn! I got crab! I got shrimps! I got 'em!" called Old Artis, the peddler. I looked up, and I was in front of the barbershop.

The bell tinkled as I opened the door. There were customers in both of the red leather chairs— Daddy's pride and joy—and he was moving from one

to the other, applying hot towels and snapping his scissors with a flourish. More customers leaned against the walls, waiting their turn.

"Where have you been, Troy?" he said, when he saw me. "I've been swamped. You know how Fridays are."

I apologized and set to work. Daddy doesn't like back-talk. I grabbed a broom from the closet and started sweeping up the multicolored cuttings that blanketed the floor.

"This is my son, Troy," Daddy said to the man whose hair he was clipping, pointing with his shears in my direction.

"That so?" rejoined the customer. I recognized him to be Lawyer Upton by the shiny patent-leather shoes he always wore. I muttered, "How do."

"How do yourself," the lawyer said, his black eyes were shrewd and cold. "I can see you've got a way with that broom. Are you planning to follow in your daddy's footsteps and be the best barber in Wilmington?"

"I don't know, sir," I muttered.

"You don't know? Do you go to school?"

"Yes, sir. The Saturday School for Colored Children."

"Fine, fine," Lawyer Upton said. "Do you want to go to college?"

"I guess so," I said. It struck me that my father was looking at me with a pleased expression on his face, slowly stirring shaving cream with his brush. I had never thought about going to college. Or even about growing up.

"Make sure that you do," the lawyer continued. "My own alma mater brought me in contact with the scions of the best black families in both Carolinas. This proved invaluable when I decided to open my office here in Wilmington. Yes, indeed, you can start from nothing, or very little, and raise yourself up to any level. This is the Golden Age for black folks, and you must grab every opportunity."

Suddenly, I heard the speaker in the graveyard shouting that the Cape Fear River would run bloody red. I shivered. Lawyer Upton might be the very lawyer that white man was despising last night.

I thought about the Cape Fear River. It was a good place, a place where Randy and I had swum and fished and gone clamming since we could walk. I couldn't imagine it blood–red.

Surely I should tell Daddy what I had seen and heard last night.

Just as I opened my mouth, a peevish voice cut in.

"Why are you filling the boy's head with such nonsense?"

The man in the other chair unwound a hot towel from his face and sat up. He turned to face Lawyer Upton almost as if he was itching for a fight.

He had a sallow complexion and pale blue eyes. That he was white didn't surprise me—many of Daddy's customers were—but that he was white and taking an interest in a black man's conversation was unusual. I didn't know what to think, and I looked to my father to show me how to act, but he was busily stroking shaving cream over the lawyer's upper lip and he didn't raise his eyes.

"You speak of a Golden Age, Mr. Upton," the white man was saying, "but let's look at our leaders today. Wilmington is about to embark on the time-honored practice of electing her leaders. Voters must decide among Democratic and Republican candidates for nine offices. Now, since Wilmington has a majority of black voters, logic would tell us that if ninety-eight percent of the blacks vote Republican, then the Republican candidates will win. Do you think that will happen? I don't."

All this talk of elections was giving me a headache. "But why not?" I burst out.

"Good question," the man said and fixed me with his pale eyes. "Because Wilmington's voting districts are unfairly divided. There are three districts. In one, the First Ward, the population is mostly Black. In the two other wards it is mostly White. Each district elects one alderman. The First Ward has three times as many voters as the other two, but it can still elect only one alderman. Do they teach you arithmetic in school? If so, even you can see how that's unjust."

"Mr. Strong, I do believe you are preparing another of your scandalous editorials," Lawyer Upton said drily. "Every time you publish one of your so-called opinions, the hardware stores do a brisk business in guns and ropes."

"Freedom of the press, Mr. Upton. I'm sure you're familiar with the idea."

"You take that right too far, however. This last issue of the *Daily Courier* will bring trouble to you and to the entire black community—mark my words. Telling people it's no worse for a black man to be intimate with a white woman than for a white man to be intimate with a black woman is going to provoke the white people in this city. We want to work with them, not against them. After all, we live here. In the words of our esteemed governor, a black man's rights are protected by law, but white men don't always heed the law."

"Then we must insure that they do! You have touched upon the very issue I discuss in this week's column. You'll be fascinated to read it, Lawyer Upton. I assert that it is as terrible for a white man to rape a black woman as it is for a black man to rape a white woman."

Daddy seemed to be ignoring the men's conversation, so intent was he on dusting the fine dark hairs from the lawyer's shoulders. But I noticed that his brows were drawn down severely.

"That'll do it, Lawyer Upton," Daddy said loudly. "I hope to see you in church this Sunday."

"Good day, Mr. Worth," Upton said, as he got out of the chair. It seemed to me that he and my father exchanged a long look when he pressed some coins into Daddy's hand.

As for the white man, Lawyer Upton completely ignored him, though he paused as he was opening the door to flip a silver nickel in my direction.

"Remember what I said, son," he drawled, and gave me a wink.

I caught the nickel but dropped the broom, and by the time I had straightened up and got back to sweeping, my father was at the next chair, working efficiently but without his usual good-humored expression.

The white man tried to meet Daddy's eye in the mirror. I noticed that he was soberly dressed, like a Yankee. His handlebar mustache was waxed at the tips.

"You must hear a great deal about the events of the day in your barbershop, Mr. Worth."

"I hear my share," my father replied. But he pressed his lips together like he tasted something sour.

"I'm sure, in that case, that you realize that there are some in this city who don't want the black community to vote in this election. They want to intimidate people so that they're afraid to go to the polls. I myself have received a threatening letter from some group called 'The Secret Nine' because I've promoted the Republican cause in my newspaper."

"Hmm," Daddy replied.

"If you hear of any trouble brewing I hope you'll let me know. I can warn people of the danger in the pages of the *Daily Courier*."

"Certainly, Mr. Strong. That'll be two bits."

"Thank you, Mr. Worth. Bye the bye, your son seems an intelligent fellow."

"Yes, indeed," Daddy said, and his face relaxed into a smile. "In some ways Troy is smart as a whip. In others, he's a mite too smart."

Strong laughed. "I need a printer's devil at my newspaper," he said. "Send this boy along next week, and I'll pay him fifty cents a week. What do you think of that, son?"

My jaw dropped. This was surely my lucky day! First a silver nickel and now a job paying two bits a week!

"That sounds fine, sir," I stammered.

He laughed again. "Good. Then I'll see you on Monday. My office is on Seventh Street, above Hurston's Saloon."

"I know the place," I said. "That's right near our church."

He nodded. The bell tinkled as the door closed

behind him.

I stopped sweeping. Mustapha Jones, who had been quietly sitting in the window sill, stepped up to the chair Mr. Strong had vacated. Shorty Clemmons, just off the night shift—he was a policeman—settled into the other chair, and there was an uncomfortable silence while Daddy tied fresh sheets around their necks. He carefully cleaned his straight razor on a towel, then sharpened it on a strop. I could hear a fly buzzing against the plate glass window. The bell tinkled as the door admitted another customer.

"Howdy, men," boomed Big Isaac. "How's life treating you all? I don't need to ask you, do I, Troy? I've already seen Troy here this morning, drinking from the horse trough with the other critters, isn't that right, son?"

Everybody laughed and the laughter just kept rolling along as Mustapha Jones, who was humpbacked and had a reedy voice that gave everything he said a comic turn, came out with, "Have you heard the news, Isaac? Troy's going to be a newspaper man."

Big Isaac looked at me in surprise, "That true? Well, just be sure you spell my name right."

"Are you going to be in the papers, Isaac? You planning a wedding—or a funeral?" Shorty Clemmons ribbed the big man.

"Both. I'm gonna bury you and marry your wife."

More laughter. Isaac turned back to me. "So, you gonna be the shrimp reporter, Troy?"

"No, sir," I said proudly. "I'm going to be a printer's devil over at the *Daily Courier*. It'll pay well, too. The only thing that worries me is that I've never yet worked for a white man, and I don't know—I'm kind of scared."

At that the whole shop burst out laughing again. I felt my cheeks grow hot.

"What's the joke?" I muttered.

"Why, son," Daddy said, "Mr. Strong isn't a white man. He's black as you and me. The *Daily Courier* is a colored paper—haven't you ever seen it?"

SHOP
TALK

B IG ISAAC WAS ROARING WITH LAUGHTER!
I didn't say anything. I just stepped outside to the dustbin. The air smelled of fall, and I stood a minute, cooling off. On the wall of the saloon next door I saw a leaflet had been pasted onto the bricks; "Beware The Secret Nine," it read. Below was a drawing of a hand holding a pistol and a skull and crossbones.

Who or what is that? I thought. *Aren't they the ones who Mr. Strong said sent him threats?*

I went back inside. Daddy was still chuckling, his scissors going snip, snip, snip, around Shorty Clemmons's head.

"Let me explain something to you, Troy," he said kindly. "Mr. Strong may look white, but his grandmother was a slave. She belonged to the governor of North Carolina, and before he died, he set her and all her children free, and left them a good-sized farm down near Raleigh. So Alex Strong and his brothers, DuMont and—what's his other brother's name, Shorty? Oh, yes, Reid—all look like white folks. But in this state, if your great–great–great–grandma was black, then you're black, too, no matter the color of your skin."

"The thing of it is," added Shorty Clemmons, "he hasn't really been accepted among black folks here-abouts, let alone the white ones. If he keeps writing editorials like the one last week, he could make things mighty hot for us in Wilmington."

"Still and all," Daddy added, "I'm proud to have the 'Only Negro Daily in the World'—that's what it says right on the front page—right here in Wilmington."

Everybody seemed to be looking to me to say something, but I just started sweeping up more hair.

Big Isaac stood up and yawned, stretching to his full length of six foot something.

"Well, I'd best be getting back to the cotton com-press," he said. He seemed to add, "School on Sunday?" as he handed my father a coin, but in so low a voice I could barely make out the words.

"Mmm-hum," said Daddy. "Watch your back."

"I don't have to," laughed Big Isaac. "My woman watches for me." The others followed him out.

It struck me as odd that I'd heard Sunday men-tioned twice in the last hour. It wasn't like Daddy was a deacon at First African Presbyterian Church. I hard-ly had time to mull that one over before a face appeared at the window that turned my blood to water. The door opened, and there stood the man I'd seen in the cemetery, calling for my people's murder. For an instant, his steel-gray eyes met mine, and then Capt'n Pinck came between us.

Pinck I knew. He was the editor of the *Wilmington Clarion*, a messy-looking, hard-drinking fellow. Summer and winter, he always wore a rumpled linen suit blotched with tobacco juice from his chew. He was carrying a knotty oak cane as thick as your arm. Once, I'd heard some truck farmers down at the depot joking about Pinhead Pinck—his head sets on his big shoulders like a tree frog setting on a fence rail—but to his face he was always Capt'n Pinck. He'd been known to use that stick of his like a club. Just the other day, Shorty had told how Pinck had horse-whipped a barkeep for serving what the Capt'n called pelican pee whiskey. He wasn't too happy, either, when Shorty arrested him.

"How do, Jimbo," Pinck said to my father. "This is Colonel Cantwell, the next mayor of our fair city. He needs a trim and a shave. And mind you do it right, boy. I've been singing your praises as a wizard of the shears."

"Step this way, sir," Daddy said, wiping a red leather chair with a towel. Daddy wasn't laughing. He didn't even nod to Shorty and Mustapha Jones as they slipped out the door. To me he barked, "Troy, get a clean cloth and wipe down the mirror."

The other man lowered himself almost warily into the chair. He crossed his legs and ran a hand down the crease of his dove-colored trousers. There was something old–fashioned and worn at the elbows about his attire but even so, I had never seen a man so finely dressed. Mr. B. Sullivan Leigh, the customs collector, had always been my model of a fine-looking gentleman. His coats were shiny and black, and his shirt collars glowed so white that you had to shade your eyes to look him in the face. But this man's waistcoat must have kept five women sewing night and day, it was so thick with embroidery. His coat looked as soft as a fine dun mare's, and just that color, too, although it was frayed somewhat at the sleeves. Looped around his neck was a silk tie, knotted in a half hitch.

I saw all this from the corner of my eye as I got the stepladder and climbed up to where I could reach the top of the mirror. Seeing this man sitting there so calm and cool, I could hardly believe he had been the wild talker of the night before.

"Did I understand Capt'n Pinck to say that you're running for mayor?" Daddy asked, as he tied a sheet around the man's neck.

"Yes, you did, boy. As a Democrat, of course."

The Colonel half turned in his chair to look my father in the eye.

"And I expect to win," he added quietly.

My father didn't say anything.

"I suppose you know that the governor is coming to Wilmington tonight, Colonel Cantwell," Capt'n Pinck remarked.

He'd sat himself in the other chair and was tapping the instep of his scuffed boots with his cane.

"It's said he wants to observe the city elections on Tuesday. Make sure all's fair and square at the polling stations." He laughed unpleasantly.

The colonel was looking into his eyes in the mirror.

"I myself consider Governor Russell the chief engineer of this plot to further the power of the Negro," he said, and the words rolled off his tongue like water down a gully. "As you so beautifully expressed it in your newspaper, Capt'n Pinck, these bold and saucy Republicans are plague-ridden parasites feeding on the failed dreams of the Confederacy. I can only hope that this election will bring a return to the democracy my forefathers and my brethren fought and died for."

I realized that my mouth was open. I stared at the man's reflection in the mirror, mesmerized.

"Yes, sir, Colonel," Pinck sniggered. "I know a fine bunch of gun-toting Democrats who are ready and willing to rid Wilmington of all kinds of Republican varmints. If I was a betting man, which I am, I'd lay even money that Governor Russell might find a party of a different kind meeting his train. A lynching party!"

He lifted his cane into firing position, quickly traversed the interior of the shop with it, then took careful aim at my back! He mimed squeezing the trigger. I shut my eyes waiting for the shot.

When I opened them again, the two men were leaving. Cantwell brushed his lapels and shoulders with fine long fingers. Capt'n Pinck slapped his broken-brimmed hat against his thigh, raising a cloud of dust, before jamming it back on his head. There was a flicker of light as the colonel flipped a coin at my father and a clink as it hit the floor and spun like a top. The door opened and closed, and they were gone.

I was still up my ladder, but I jumped down when I saw my father move to the window. Side by side, we watched the men cross Dock Street.

Somebody else was watching the scene from the sidewalk, and he turned to look through the window at Daddy and me. It was Randy.

He lifted his hand timidly.

My father reached up and jerked down the shade.

"Come on, Troy, we're closing early," he said. He flipped the sign on the door to Closed. With quick, sharp movements, he took off his barbering coat and hung it on its hook. He motioned me outside, locked the door, and took off down the street.

"Daddy!" I called, "Wait for me."

He didn't even turn around. I watched as he took a right on Front Street and began threading his way through the crowds, dodging a streetcar and a heavy wagon loaded with kegs of beer. I looked around for Randy, but he had disappeared.

Sidestepping big-shouldered dockworkers and big-skirted housewives, I tagged along a block or so behind Daddy. By the time he had got to Ann Street, it struck me that he walked like a scissors, throwing out his legs without bending them. I imagined he was cutting up the road like he cut hair: snip, snip, snip.

When Daddy reached Sixth Street, I decided he was going home, but he took a left and slipped into the gate of Lawyer Upton's big house. He held it open with one hand and gestured at me impatiently. I ran the rest of the way.

"Troy, I've got business here. I want you to run like blazes to King's Cotton Compress and give a message to Big Isaac. Don't talk to anybody else, you hear? Just Isaac. Say, 'There's a camp meeting tonight.' Got that?"

"Yes, sir."

"Good. Now go!"

MESSAGES

I TOOK OFF RUNNING, AND BEFORE LONG I WAS IN PATTY'S Hollow, the warehouse district that lies along the Cape Fear River. I could see the water glimmering between the big sooty buildings. I whipped by the Cotton Exchange, passed Byrd & Byrd's wholesale grocery warehouse, and there it was rearing up against the sky: King's Cotton Compress.

The compress used to be a customs house before the war, but the Kings had bought it from an old family gone to pot. People said they were making money hand over fist. They were Yankees. They didn't go to church like regular folks did but had service on Saturdays. They were good to all their workers, though, and seemed to like black folks more than most white people. I'd heard Big Isaac boast of going to their big house on Princess Street for dinner.

Outside the building, women in calico headscarves and men in ragged straw hats were unloading bushel baskets of raw white cotton from a train car. One woman with a fresh-looking scar on her cheek caught my eye, and I followed her into the huge warehouse.

"Peggy Ace," I yelled over the noise of the compress. "Hey, you, Peggy!" The scraps of cotton in the air looked like snow.

Peggy Ace looked back over her shoulder, then dumped her basket of cotton onto a long table piled with the stuff.

"Hey, you," she said. Her words slow and thick.

I tried not to stare at the scar shaped like a big lopsided teardrop just below her right eye. It looked almost like a cattle brand. She must have gotten into some kind of accident, I thought.

"I'm looking for Big Isaac."

There was a flicker of life in her eyes when she jerked her head toward the back of the warehouse. "He's supervising."

I made my way past all the people sorting cotton at the long tables. They were gossiping and telling stories through the clouds of cotton dust. When I got to where the compress machines stood, there was too much noise for talking.

The compresses were steam presses that flattened the piles of fluffy cotton into something like a rug. These rugs could be folded, tied with burlap and rope, and loaded onto Mr. King's steamship for delivery to Baltimore or New York or even England.

"Howdy, Troy!" Isaac yelled. He was watching a skinny man spread cotton on the bed of the machine.

"You looking for another job?"

I dodged a burst of scalding steam. Pulling Isaac aside, I stood on tiptoe to get closer to his ear.

"Daddy told me to find you," I said, in a low voice. "There's a camp meeting tonight."

Big Isaac's eyes darted around to see if anybody had overheard me.

He said softly, "I understand. Now, I want you to take the same message to Mr. Ebenezer Zadoc, the man who owns Zadoc's store."

I nodded. Mr. Zadoc was a carpetbagger. People whispered that he'd marched with General Sherman and helped burn Savannah. He'd come to Wilmington after the war and sold liquor to the occupying Union soldiers. Made a mint of money. Now he owned the biggest general store in town and sold everything to everybody.

Big Isaac bent almost double so that he could look me in the face. "Now be careful when you're downtown, Troy. There's a Democratic rally at the opera house tonight, and the Red Shirts will be making meanness in the streets. After you give Mr. Zadoc the message, you run straight home, and no dawdling."

"The Red Shirts?"

"Vigilantes," he said. "Stay clear of them. They're just looking for an excuse to shoot somebody."

"I hear you," I said, and I ran outside. As I passed the train car, a strong hand grabbed my shoulder. I looked up into Peggy Ace's scarred face.

"Boy!" she said. "You have some news for me?"

"No, ma'am."

Her hand was squeezing my shoulder like a vice.

"Don't forget, now. If anything happens to Isaac,
Peggy Ace will come looking for you to find out why."

That didn't make any sense, but she was staring
down at me like a snake considering supper, so I nodded. She loosened her grip.

I took off again down Nutt Street, across Water
Street, to the Front. As always, my heart lifted when I
considered the river. The hustle, noise, and strange car-
goes piled on the dock, and the cursing dockmen and
sailors were thrilling. I saw a brown pelican sitting on a
piling, soaking up the sunshine and waiting for a fisher-
man to throw down some fish guts or rotten bait.

Pelicans are gawky, awkward creatures, but they'll hurl themselves on a fish like a cannonball. Randy and I used to borrow a canoe from the rows of those tied up along the banks and take off downriver. We'd fish all day and come home sunburned and hungry. My momma or his would fry up our catch with a little cornmeal and flour. Mrs. Hollis was sweet to me. I remember her talking to Momma one day in the yard. She picked a tulip bud from one of her trees and put it in my momma's hair. "Here, Adelle," she had said. "Isn't this pretty?"

The hurt in Randy's eyes when Daddy pulled down the window shade popped into my mind, and I picked up my pace. Rushing past the marine supply stores, the pawn shops, the cigar stores, and the sailor's hotels, I came to Zadoc's General Store. The plate glass windows reflected the street back at me. An American flag hanging above the double doors snapped in the breeze like gunfire.

Inside, Zadoc's store was filled with house servants doing last-minute shopping before lunchtime. I weaved through the pyramids of canned peaches and sardines, and tables stacked with bolts of cloth and blue jeans, to an iron staircase at the back of the store. Mr. Zadoc's office, a platform with walls, was at the top. It overlooked the store so that he could see who bought what and eavesdrop on the gossip. If he heard something he disagreed with, he would lean over and shout down his opinion. People thought this was rude, but his prices were so good that everybody still came to shop.

I remember last July 4th celebration. The mayor

was just finishing his speech, and everybody was clapping when Mr. Zadoc pushed his way through the crowd, jumped onto the grandstand and started to sing, "Mine Eyes Have Seen the Glory."

The white people booed and carried on. Daddy and the Etheridges and the mayor and Mr. Heeks and the Kings and some others started singing. The hecklers just packed up and left us there. We sang all the verses.

As I reached the head of the spiral staircase, I could see him through the window. He was running his finger along the columns in a big ledger. I knocked on the glass, and he gestured me in.

"Do I know you, son?" he asked, eyeing me suspiciously over his half glasses.

"No, sir. My name is Troy Worth. My daddy owns the barbershop on Dock Street. I have a message for you."

"From your daddy?"

"No, sir, from Big Isaac Samuels. He told me to tell you there was a camp meeting tonight."

He regarded me speculatively. "Anything else?"

"No, sir."

"Tell me something, then. Do you like candy?"

"Yes, sir."

"Tell Mabel down at the counter to give you ten cents' worth of licorice. Then I want you to do something for me. I want you to run over to the Saturday School and give Miss Morris a message. Tell her 'E Pluribus Unum.' Say that after me."

I did, and he dismissed me with a wave of his hand.

I sighed and headed down the stairs. I was tired.

These people had me running like a rabbit.

A long rope of raspberry licorice revived me, and I was walking—I'd given up running—along, when I saw three white boys up ahead carrying fishing poles.

"Hey, you, Randy!" I called out.

Randy turned his head and saw me. He murmured something to his friends, and they laughed in an ugly, jeering way.

"I saw you at the barbershop," he said, as if he was telling something on me.

"You know I've been working for my daddy."

"Yeah," an underfed towhead, announced. "Coloreds have to work so they don't get into mischief. Isn't that right, Randy?"

The two boys and Randy were standing in a half circle watching me, waiting to see what I would do.

"Haven't I seen you boys before?" I said, real casual and smooth. "You're always playing by the swinging doors at Isley's Saloon. Your daddy gets thrown out of there regularly, doesn't he? Like the trash."

"Shut up, you negrah!" the third boy screamed and he jumped at me.

"Bockra!" I yelled, and put my head down so that he ran right into it with his belly. That took the wind out of his sails. I kicked him hard in the thighs and butt, and I could feel bone under my boot. The boy got on his hands and knees and then scurried, half crawling, down the street. His brother took off after him.

"Listen, Randy," I said, and I took hold of the sleeve of his worn blue jacket. "Something bad is going on. Those boys you're hanging around with haven't ever bothered me before. What's wrong with you? Why're you palling around with such trash? Why was your daddy at that meeting in the cemetery last night? Those men want to murder black people. They want to run us out of town. How come your daddy wants to do that to us? Aren't we neighbors? Aren't you and I friends?"

Randy avoided my eyes. He kicked at the dust with his bare toe.

"I don't know, Troy," he said. "Don't ask me. Poppa says things are going to change soon and be better for us. He says the colored people have kept all the carpentry and brick laying and ship building jobs to themselves, and that there's nothing a white man can do to get work. But he says it will be different after Election Day."

He still wouldn't look me in the face. I felt like there was a stone in my chest, stopping me from taking a deep breath. I was so confused that I didn't know whether to punch Randy in the face or burst out crying. I had to find out what all this was about. I began to think that all these mysterious messages I was delivering were tied into that ring of fire.

"Randy, I'm going to find out what's really going on in Wilmington whether you help me or not."

I was aching for him to be the old Randy and clap me on the back and say, "Surely, Brother Troy! It's a conspiracy, that's what it is, and we'll figure out the whole thing and be heroes!"

But the old Randy would have helped me fight those boys, not stood there and watched.

Neither of us said another word until we came up to the little whitewashed schoolhouse. It had two doors with two little landings, one for girls and one for boys. I paused at the boys' door, and said, "You want to wait? We could walk home together."

"Okey-doke," said Randy.

I found Miss Morris marking papers at her desk. She smiled when she saw me. She was from Philadelphia, too, just like the Kings, and she always wore gray or black dresses, even during the dog days of September, and a little white cap on her head.

"So there's my prize student. Don't tell me you need some help with your homework."

"No, ma'am. I have a message from Mr. Zadoc. He said for me to tell you 'E Pluribus Unum.'"

It seemed to me that Miss Morris went as white as her white cap. Her hand went to her mouth, and she muttered something to herself. I began backing down the aisle between the benches. I'd just about gotten to the door when she jumped out of her chair and came after me.

"Troy, I'm glad you came to see me. Listen, if anything happens to you or your family, you come and find me. I'll do what I can. Now, go straight home. I'll see you in school on Saturday."

"Yes, ma'am," I said.

I opened the door, and Randy fell forward into the floor. He jumped up, red-faced, and leaped down the steps into the street.

Miss Morris folded her hands and looked cross.

45

"Is this a friend of yours, Troy?" she asked.

"Yes, ma'am," I muttered. "This is Randy Hollis."

"Well, Randy Hollis, you're old enough to know better than to listen at keyholes. Come inside if you're interested in the school. We always have room for a boy willing to learn."

"I ain't going to no colored school," he said. "Besides, my poppa can't read and he says I don't need to, either. And we don't need Yankees like you telling us what to do, and lording it over us, offering us hand-outs and charity like we was negrahs! Once we get your kind out of Wilmington, things'll be good for us again—and bad for you!"

I felt the blood rush to my head. For a minute I could hardly see. It was as though the sky had gone dark.

"That's foolish talk," Miss Morris said sternly. "We fought a war to end that kind of thinking. Education is for black and white children. In my school, anybody who wants to learn is welcome." With a rustle of skirts she turned to go back inside.

"Remember, Randy Hollis," she added, in a more gentle tone. "The door is always open."

Randy stood there, his mouth twisting. Then he bolted, running crookedly down the street like a lame dog.

Miss Morris and I stared after him. She didn't say a word. Neither did I.

THE RED
SHIRTS RIDE

WHEN DADDY DIDN'T SHOW UP FOR SUPPER, I COULD TELL that Momma was worried. She'd made his favorite meal, seasoning the turnip greens with a little pork left over from the Heeks's dinner, and frying some breaded catfish and sliced potatoes. All the time Callie and I were eating, she didn't even sit down. She just watched us, her hand pulling at the skin of her throat. I was reaching for my second triangle of cornbread when she said, "Troy, did anything happen at the barbershop today?"

"Well, Daddy did close early to go see Lawyer Upton."

Her eyes widened. She had that expression on her face she gets when the postman brings a letter: bad news.

"I want you to run down to the shop right now,"

she said, "and see if your father is there. Then come right back and let me know, you hear?"

"Yes, Momma."

I took the cornbread with me and ate as I walked.

It was a beautiful evening. The sky was purple and rose, like the colors in the glass windows at church. As if by magic, the streetlights began to light up all over the downtown. Surely I was the luckiest boy alive, to be living in such a fine city! Someday I would be a big man in this town, a captain of a steamship or a lawyer or maybe even customs collector, and live in a fine house with servants and a horse and carriage.

But then I remembered Randy and I didn't feel so happy anymore.

The shade still covered the window of the barbershop, but there was a light on inside. Shadows moved across the blind like a pantomime.

I knelt down at the door and peeked through the keyhole. There was Daddy in front of the mirror, and Big Isaac beside him, then Lawyer Upton beside the gaslight, and Mustapha Jones, and Shorty Clemmons. Leaning against the wall were Mr. Heeks and Mr. Zadoc. Closest to the door, I recognized the round moonish face of Turps Etheridge, our neighbor.

"What we need to do is save ourselves," Lawyer Upton was saying. "Let's get Alex Strong to leave town. Then we'll tell the White Government Union that the black community never supported the *Daily Courier* in any way. We owe it to our families to do whatever we

can to avoid trouble."

Some men, my daddy included, nodded in agreement, while Big Isaac and Turps Etheridge started to argue with the lawyer.

Turps must have felt my eye on him, because the next thing I knew, the door had been jerked open and Turps had me by the arm.

"What you doing on your knees, boy?" he jeered, pulling me inside. "Have you lost something in that keyhole?"

"Why are you here, Troy?" Daddy demanded.

"Momma sent me to find you! She was worried."

"Well, get back home right now—and stay there!"

"Hang on a minute, Worth," Mr. Zadoc interrupted. "Now that the boy's here, let's use our horse sense. Weren't we just saying we needed to find out what was happening at the Democratic rally? Well, here's somebody who could slip into the opera house and find out."

"A black boy wouldn't be safe at a Democratic rally. The White Government Union has Red Shirts patrolling the streets, and all God fearing citizens are staying in their homes," cautioned Lawyer Upton. "I'm not ashamed to admit that I hesitate at the thought of traversing the city after dark."

"No, sir," said Big Isaac, "the lawyer's right. This is a man's job. I'll go. I'll walk in the front door of that opera house and ask them what they plan to do. Anybody who tries to stop me can talk to Sue Belle." He took a pistol out of his belt and held it out for everybody to see.

"Put that firearm away, Isaac," Mr. Zadoc said. He looked at me as if he expected me to speak.

"I'll do it," I said, "I know how to slip into the basement of the opera house and get in under the stage near the orchestra pit. Nobody will see me. Just tell me what you're planning. What's going on?"

"Troy," said Daddy. He pulled me away from Mr. Zadoc. "You'll do nothing of the kind. Go home right this instant."

"I want to help," I protested.

"Troy." It was just one word, but I knew my daddy meant me to obey. I turned and walked out of the shop. I shut the door carefully behind me, lingering just a minute, hoping to hear something more. But there was silence inside. I knew they were waiting until I was gone before recommencing their meeting.

I began to walk down Front Street. I hadn't gone more than a few yards when I heard a ruckus. I could hear people cheering. The music of a fife and drum made my blood race. Dust clouds were rising in the street up ahead.

Ducking back into the darkened doorway of the Thacker Casket Company, I decided to watch the parade.

First came the musicians in embroidered uniforms, playing a marching song. Then came a team of mules pulling the Wilmington Infantry's new Gatling gun. This excited me all the way down to my toes. To think! That thing could fire 600 rounds in a minute!

A hay wagon was brimming with white girls in

frilly dresses with red sashes. They laughed and waved and called out to the men who ran alongside.

Following the wagon rode columns of severe looking men on horseback and then about thirty men marching under a banner that read *White Government Union.* They all wore red shirts of flannel or calico or silk. I knew they must be the vigilantes Big Isaac had warned me about. Some had strips of white cloth tied over one shoulder and around the waist. All of them carried rifles. In the light of the setting sun, their faces were crimson.

Just for a minute I felt cornered and panicked. I very nearly broke cover and ran right into the middle of them. There's no doubt in my mind that they would have shot me down in the street like a rabbit.

I struggled to get hold of myself. The tail end of the parade was passing now: a passel of barefooted boys, most of them wearing red shirts. Among these was Randy Hollis. His shirt was patched and faded, but he was a rooster among hens, strutting along with his shoulders back. In his arms he cradled a beat-up rifle.

My knees gave out, and I leaned back against the locked door and shut my eyes.

When I looked again, the procession had turned up Queen Street and was heading for Dry Pond, the poorest part of town. I felt mean. I wanted to follow Randy and hurt him.

I tracked the parade like a scout, ducking from doorway to doorway as it moved further down Queen

Street, and the warehouses and marine supply stores gave way to ramshackle shacks. This was where the poorest black people lived and the skinny Irish fresh off the boat. Most of the Irish came here for work, but there wasn't enough work to go around, so they moved down to Charleston or up to Baltimore, shipping out on barges and ferries. The ones too poor or too sluggish to do that ended up in Dry Pond.

As the Red Shirts passed along the road, the Dry Ponders came out on their front porches to watch—women mostly, with children at their skirts. A man stepped into the street, but moved back hastily when one of the riders kicked his horse into a canter and swerved towards him. All the Red Shirts laughed and cheered.

At Fourth Street the procession turned away from the river, and I ran up Third Street as fast as my legs could carry me. I figured the parade was going to end up at the opera house and I'd better be inside before it got there.

The Lyric is reckoned to be the finest opera house in the Carolinas. There are four tall columns out front, and inside it's all curving balconies, velvet curtains, and gilded sea shells and oak leaves. Daddy brought me in the front door once just to show me how splendid it was. It had been built by black contractors and plasterers and builders, he said. Not many black people went to performances there—the tickets cost too much—but Lawyer Upton did, and Mr. B. Sullivan Leigh.

Randy and I had discovered a little window with a broken lock. We had sneaked into the basement with some other kids from the neighborhood and seen a thing or two my momma wouldn't have liked. Once we saw a woman singing, her arms bare as a fancy lady's.

I sneaked around to the back of the building and, sure enough, the window swung open with a little push. I squeezed through, leaped down into the dark basement, and felt my way along a wall to a curving metal staircase. Stationed up the stairs, I could look through an opening at the front of the stage.

I counted nine pairs of feet moving around the stage. One pair of particularly wrinkled trousers I pegged as belonging to Capt'n Pinck. The house was filling up; I could hear people exchanging greetings, coughing, and chuckling.

Then, all of the men on the stage moved to a table draped with a blood-colored cloth emblazoned with an open eye. Capt'n Pinck's wrinkled trousers stepped up to a podium.

"Quiet, boys!" Pinck yelled. He slapped his open hand on the podium.

A lull fell.

"Listen up!" Pinck continued. "I want you to give a big Democratic welcome to our next mayor!"

Cheers so loud I could feel them through the floor.

"Now, you all know him and you all know his family—they're so poor now they must have been one of Wilmington's finest families before the war!"

Laughter. Pinck turned back toward the table.

"Just a joke, Colonel, just a joke. Without further ado, let me present Colonel Cantwell, the man who will redeem our fair city—and further our most noble designs!"

Cheers. Pinck's legs disappeared and some fine grey trousers stepped up to the podium.

"Silence, gentlemen. Silence!" The voice rang out like the pealing of a bell.

"We meet tonight on the eve of Wilmington's elections," he said. "God willing, after tomorrow we will no longer have a dirty Republican as mayor and scalawags and carpetbaggers in the other city offices. Sitting before you on this stage are the Democratic candidates for those nine offices."

There were roars of approval. The men at the table rose and bowed.

"I don't have to tell you that the colored people have conspired to gain complete control of Wilmington's government," Cantwell continued. "Newspapers up and down the coast have reported on the very real danger North Carolina faces of becoming a black colony. This is what Yankee Reconstruction has brought us. The colored man is in the saddle. His hand is firm upon the reins. His horse is the white man. Will you be ridden?"

The crowd shouted, "No, No!" I sank down deeper in my hiding place until all I could see of the speaker were his polished boots.

"By now you have read the editorial published in the *Daily Courier* today, an editorial condoning—nay, encouraging!—the rape of white women. Am I to understand that the author of this filth is still breathing the same air as our wives and daughters? Is there no able-bodied Anglo–Saxon who can still aim and fire his gun? Has the world come to an end? Or will you join with me in making this Republican scoundrel wish that it had?"

The crowd went wild with long whooping Rebel yells. The floor shook with the sound of hundreds of feet stamping.

I knew I had to get out of there before they smelled me out like an animal. I leaped downstairs, felt my way through the dark basement, and squeezed through the little window.

Once outside, I took a deep breath and looked toward the front entrance. A throng of people were gathered there, still trying to get inside. The speech-making was continuing.

I headed for home. Daddy might stay late at the barbershop, and I wanted to get back and let Momma know I had seen him. She was probably out of her mind with worrying about us. I kept to the shade of the big trees lining the streets, hoping nobody would see me.

Behind me horses neighed and men shouted, and then somebody fired shots into the air. I froze. I looked down Third Street where some barrels of burning tar gave off enough light to reveal armed sentries idling at the cross streets.

There was going to be trouble for sure.

A DECLARATION OF INDEPENDENCE

THE NIGHT SEEMED SO QUIET, AND YET THERE WAS DANGER somewhere in the darkness. I felt eerie, like I was already dead, a ghost coming back to haunt somebody. I slipped along the sidewalk under the thick overhang of trees lining Fifth Avenue. My ears were pricked for the sound of gunshots. Occasionally, a lone horseman galloped by, but nobody seemed to notice me. I breathed a little more regularly and felt the weight of my arms and legs again. I moved out of the shadows.

I'd just come alongside an ornate iron gate when I heard a loud caterwaul, and suddenly a crowd of the Red Shirts was circling around me. Their horses pranced skittishly on the sidewalk, while the men howled at me.

A man reined in his horse with one hand. In the other, he held a rifle. He struggled to get the stock securely under his arm so that he could aim at me, but he was so drunk that the rifle kept slipping.

"Watch it there, Dowd, you're liable to shoot yourself out of the saddle, if you ain't careful!" one of the men jeered.

"Why you scalawag," Dowd yelled. "I'll eat your liver with my eggs before I let you—"

I wasn't going to hang around and hear more. I lunged forward and punched the horse square in the neck. It jumped, all four hooves in the air, and I was over the iron gate before it landed.

"Hey-o!" a man yelled. There was a bang, and the sudden stench of gunpowder. I glanced over my shoulder and saw the horse rear and the drunk man fall back like a rag doll, one foot caught in the stirrup.

I didn't look back anymore. I just kept running.

WHEN I BURST IN THROUGH THE BACK DOOR, THE FIRST thing I noticed was that there was a light in the parlor. Momma was sitting on the parlor sofa, wearing her robe, her hair in braids around her head. Callie was slumped beside her, snoring lightly.

"Where've you been, Troy?" she whispered fiercely. "Where's your daddy?"

"Isn't he here?"

Just then we heard Daddy's heavy tread in the kitchen. He came into the room, seemingly surprised to see us awake.

"Adelle, are you still up?"

"It isn't likely I'm going to get my beauty rest

with you two fools out getting yourselves killed, am I?" Momma snapped.

"Now, now," he said, "it isn't as bad as that. Just drunks shooting at their shadows."

"Don't you 'now, now' me," Momma retorted. "You strut around as if the good Lord had met you around the corner and divulged all the mysteries of the world. It seems like half the world's got a secret and the other half is scared they going to find out what it is. All day today, Mrs. Heeks jumped out of her skin every time I put a lid on a pot. I nearly burned up their pie this evening, she got me so nervous. Then this young 'uns gallivanting around to all hours. James Worth, something is going on in this town. Now, what is it?"

Daddy sunk down into an armchair. He put his hands over his eyes and rubbed his whole face like it was a cloudy mirror.

"A letter was delivered tonight at the barbershop, Adelle. Along the top of the paper was *Wilmington Declaration of Independence* and along the bottom *The Secret Nine.*"

"The Secret Nine," interrupted my mother. "What kind of foolishness is that?"

"It isn't foolishness, Adelle. At least, not the childish kind. The letter was addressed to the most prominent men in the black community by name, and it drew out a new plan for Wilmington. No office-holding, no schools, no voting, no nothing for Negroes. White laborers are to be employed before blacks. Big

Isaac would be fired from the compress, and Shorty from the police. The *Daily Courier* is to be packed up and shipped out of the city, and Mr. Alex Strong with it."

"What? Are they going to start the war up again?"

"That's what we've been trying to find out, honey. We looked at the letter upside, downside, and this side of Tuesday, and we can't figure how they mean to go about enforcing this 'declaration.' We all decided we'd do anything to avoid violence. So we drafted a letter—me, Lawyer Upton, Mr. Zadoc, and the Reverend Pyle—and gave it to Lawyer Upton to deliver to Pinck's paper, the *Clarion*. Mr. Zadoc is going to telegraph the governor, tell him that we may need troops here on Election Day.

"Soldiers are coming back to Wilmington?" Momma gasped.

Daddy gave a dry chuckle. "We're gonna need soldiers just to deal with Big Isaac. He's determined to fight anybody and everybody by himself. It seems there was some unpleasantness about a certain woman." He gave Momma a knowing look. "Anyhow, we've got to head off a riot before it's too late."

"Riot!" Momma cried, so loudly that Callie's eyes opened in confusion.

"What did the letter say, Daddy?" I asked. "Are you going to go warn Mr. Strong yourself?"

Daddy turned to look at me. His face closed up tight.

"What's this I hear about you being out at all hours? Didn't you come home as I told you to?"

I didn't like the way this was heading, so I said, "But what about the Secret Nine, Daddy?"

"That's none of your concern, son," Momma said with a quaver in her voice. Her hands were fluttering over the collar of her robe. "I don't want you getting involved in something as ugly as all this. Leave it to your elders to work out. Now come here and help me lift up your sister."

THE DAILY COURIER

DADDY LEFT BEFORE THE REST OF US WERE UP. AT BREAKFAST we all three moved like sleepwalkers. Momma's face was an ashen gray.

"Eat up, children," she said automatically. "You've got to get to school. Troy, your daddy said for you to come home afterward with Callie. He doesn't need you to work today."

Saturday was Momma's half-day at the Heeks's, but she still had to be there to cook the breakfast. She hurried off before we'd finished eating.

Callie was quiet on the way to school, and she brought Euphonia, her rag doll, along with her. She doesn't usually carry her doll around.

"Aren't you afraid you'll get teased carrying that doll?" I asked her. "You're no thumb–sucking baby."

I expected a punch on the arm or at least some

smart sass, but Callie just shrugged.

"What's wrong, baby sister?" I asked. "You look as low as a grasshopper's gaiters."

"Nobody's telling me anything," she said. "I know you're out running around and finding things out, and Daddy is too, and what do I do? Sit home."

"That's 'cause you're a girl, bonehead."

"I know that! But it isn't fair!"

I could see the schoolhouse just ahead. Miss Morris was standing on the little porch ringing a handbell.

"Well, this is where I get off, sweetie pie."

"What? Aren't you going to school?"

"No, ma'am. I've got bigger fish to fry."

Well, that tore it.

"Troy Worth!" Callie yelled. "I'm going to tell Daddy on you and when he gets finished with your behind you aren't going to sit down for a week!"

I laughed and started running backward, waving at her. I laughed even harder when she got so mad that she threw her doll down in the street and started kicking dirt after me.

I headed over to Hurston's Saloon, not really sure of my plan. Something was driving me to go see Mr. Strong. I passed the First African Presbyterian Church, with its fine white steeple and the bell the congregation had bought just last year. Next door was the saloon, with its frosted glass and swinging doors. From the upstairs window hung a sign: *The Daily Courier*.

I ran up the staircase at the back of the building and rapped on the door. It opened an inch.

"Yes?"

It was Mr. Strong himself, peering through the crack of the door.

"I'm Troy Worth, Mr. Strong. You told me to come and work for you."

His pale eyes were cold. "I asked you to come next week."

"Uh, yes, sir, you did. But I heard about the letter and wondered if—"

"What letter?"

"About you having to leave Wilmington."

He frowned. "Come in."

I stepped inside, and he locked the door behind me.

"My brothers have already gone," he said. "I've decided to stick it out. After all, the White Government Union has had copies of my editorials distributed all over the South. They hope to whip up public sentiment, no doubt, so that they can lynch me with impunity. But I refuse to run like a whipped dog. If I do, no one will credit my ideas. The bigots will have won. And I will not stand for that."

"You're not leaving?" I gasped.

"No, the Monday edition of the *Daily Courier* will be printed and ready for distribution, even if I have to do it myself. And because my brothers have so hurriedly departed, I will," he added ruefully.

"I'll help you." I knew that this was why I had come. I wanted to fight the Red Shirts, and I had known from the first time I saw him that Mr. Strong was a fighter.

He considered me expressionlessly. "Good," he said.

We were standing in a large room of bare brick. There was a big printing press in one corner surrounded by trays of something that glinted in the sun. Bound newspapers were piled in every corner, high as towers. There were three desks. One was covered with scraps of paper and little cartoons, another with letters, and the third, very neat, had only a green blotter and a wire basket labeled *Out.*

"I was doing the paste up," he said. "Let me show you how to set type, and you can prepare the first page."

I followed him over to the press. He lifted up one of the little wooden trays and showed me that each one was filled with squares of polished metal bearing the raised outline of a letter or punctuation mark. My job was to clean the type, which meant that I took the slivers of metal and rubbed the ink off them with a cotton rag. Then Mr. Strong would spell out a word for me, and I would drop the correct pieces of type into another little tray.

I'd learned how to spell and do sums at school, but I'd never known of anybody using language the way Mr. Strong did. The way he talked about the Secret Nine made the hair on the back of my neck draw in. He believed the Secret Nine was conniving to keep the black community away from the polls, and to get Mr. Strong out of town and the newspaper closed down. If they managed to scare all the Republicans enough, they would win the elections and things would be mighty bad for all of us.

As I spelled out every word of his editorial as he directed me, there was an uncomfortable question floating in the back of my head. What, I wondered, would my daddy say about Mr. Strong's ideas? I couldn't say why, but I knew Daddy wouldn't like what the newspaper said.

It was a long day, but we finally "put the newspaper to bed" (as Mr. Strong put it), which meant that we had set all the type and had only to print the actual papers. I knew I had to go. Callie would be home from school already, which meant that Momma surely knew that I'd played hookey. I dreaded her tongue-lashing as much as the whipping Daddy would give me.

"Good work, son," Mr. Strong said, and he clapped me on the shoulder. There was even a hint of a smile on his face. "Why don't you run downstairs and get us something to eat. Here's a dollar. I'll start printing the front page."

I couldn't say no.

I pushed through the swinging doors and stepped inside Hurston's, savoring the wonderful smell of a saloon: stale cigar smoke, sawdust, sour liquor, and cubes of blue pool chalk. It took my eyes a minute to adjust to the darkness.

I leaned against the bar and looked around the room.

The place was just beginning to fill up with a Saturday night crowd of railroad workers and pickers from the truck farms. The baize-topped tables were empty, by and large, but there was a crowd around the pool table and the player piano. I noticed a man in a white suit and a panama hat, sitting alone in a dark corner. It was Capt'n Pinck.

I turned real fast, hoping he hadn't seen me. But after a minute of staring at the rows of whiskey bottles, it occurred to me that he wouldn't know me anyway. Slowly, I looked over his way. A man in a tweed jacket had stepped up to his table: Randy's father. The two men were talking, and Mr. Hollis was gesturing wildly with his beer mug.

"Troy."

I like to have jumped out of my skin. "Oh, it's you, Mr. Strong!"

"Yes. I forgot to ask you to buy me a bottle of beer. Printing is thirsty work."

The barkeep waved. "How're you keeping, Mr. Strong?"

"Fair to middling, Sodie," the editor said. He was heading out the door when Mr. Hollis noticed him.

"Spawn of Satan!" he yelled, "crawling about like a snake on your belly! You turn my guts to bile!"

Mr. Strong stopped and stared. I don't think he knew what to make of the man's curses. When he did speak, it was to Capt'n Pinck.

"My compliments on the latest issue of the *Clarion*, Capt'n," Strong called out boldly. "Once again you have succeeded in appealing to the lowest instincts of the worst element. You, sir, have elevated rabble-rousing to an art form."

Pinck was a poker player. I could tell that by the

way his face got so blank all of a sudden.

"The *Clarion* expresses the views of the white man. I wouldn't expect you to understand them, boy."

Mr. Hollis had been rocking back and forth on his heels, listening to the exchange with some impatience, but the insult in Pinck's comment hit him like a mule kick.

"Ha, ha!" He burst out in a big, drawn-out belly laugh. Capt'n Pinck joined in with a chuckle, and pretty soon some of the men standing around the pool table were guffawing.

Mr. Strong's sallow cheeks flushed a mottled red. His hand strayed to the waxed tips of his mustache.

"No, Capt'n Pinck, I understand you all too well," he said. He strode outside, leaving the double doors to swing closed behind him.

I didn't know where to look. I felt ashamed but excited. I wasn't sure if Mr. Strong had lost the battle or won it.

Sodie rushed up with some paper-wrapped sandwiches, a bottle of beer, and a bottle of sarsaparilla.

"These are on the house," he said to me. "Tell Mr. Strong I'm ashamed of that trash over there. We advertise in the *Daily Courier*," he added, "and appreciate Mr. Strong's business."

I thanked the man and headed outside. My stomach was so empty that it was rumbling like thunderheads.

But what I saw on the street made me forget about eating.

THE
CONFLAGRATION

HURSTON'S SALOON WAS SITUATED IN THE MIDDLE OF SEVENTH Street between Church and Nun. The First African Presbyterian Church was on the corner of Church and Seventh, and when I stepped out on the sidewalk I noticed a gathering of white men in front of it. It was a ragtaggle bunch of overgrown boys in overalls and men in suits—clerks from the customs house and the dry goods stores. Mixed in among these were Red Shirts. Some were carrying pieces of stove wood. Others had rifles and pistols. What struck me as the most threatening thing about the group was how quiet they all were, as if they were waiting for a signal.

A swarm of barefoot children playing kick-the-can in the alleyway beside the saloon broke up as I moved towards the *Courier*'s staircase.

"Hey," a little girl said to me, her eyes like

saucers, "something's happening."

I nodded and thrust the sandwiches into her hands. Her hungry little face lit up like a blaze of heat lightning. I took the stairs two at a time and banged on the door.

"Mr. Strong, Mr. Strong!" I hollered. "You've got to get out of here!"

I was banging so hard on the glass pane that it cracked. Mr. Strong jerked open the door.

"They're here?" he asked.

"Yes, sir, a gang of 'em. They're in front of the church. We've got to run."

He shook his head.

"But you've got to! What use are you to anybody dead? We can hide you until it's safe to skip town!"

A roar came from the street. The signal had been given. I heard thumps, as if the building was being pelted with rocks. Then a pealing voice called out, "Alex Strong, the Redemption is here! Prepare thyself to meet thy maker!"

The mob was howling, "Lynch him!" and "Fumigate the *Daily Courier*!"

"Come with me!" I pleaded, taking him by the arm. "Do you have your gun?"

He shook his head again, and a smile played around his lips. "I don't own a gun."

He looked back over his shoulder at the mess of papers around the printing press. "I haven't finished Monday's edition."

"Come on!" I begged. I pulled him down the

stairs, and I didn't let go of his arm until we had
slipped behind the church.

"Follow me," I whispered, and threw myself over
the stone wall into the cemetery. We leapt over the
graves until we came to the far corner. Now that he
was away from the office, Mr. Strong seemed to understand the danger he was in. He was hot on my heels.
We jumped the far wall, too, and landed all in a heap in
the garden of a little frame house.

We ducked under a barbed wire fence and took
off running up Eighth Street. Finally, we slowed, and I
risked a glance toward the newspaper office. Some
men were on the roof and had taken the sign off its
hinge. They cast it down on the ground like something

dirty. A cheer went up when it smashed into pieces.

"Look at that, Troy," Alex Strong said quietly. "That is how a mob responds to a new idea. This is an end to freedom in this city for a long time—perhaps forever."

I turned to look at him. I could feel tears in the corners of my eyes. "Tell me, Mr. Strong," I pleaded, "what is going to happen to us?"

But before he could reply, a white-haired woman wearing a rusty old dress the color of red cabbage rushed past us. She let out a scream: "Fire! Fire! The church is on fire!"

My eyes focused on the First African Presbyterian Church's steeple. Flames were shooting up from the belfry. I heard a ping as a bullet bounced off the big bell.

Ker–BLAM—a huge crash. The *Courier*'s printing press came out the window, one piece at a time through billowing smoke.

Mr. Strong let out a strangled sound halfway between a laugh and a sob.

More and more men on horseback joined the advance on Seventh Street. Sure as the world, somebody was going to see us if we didn't move fast, so we crawled under a hedge at the northern end of St. Luke's Street and tried to make a plan.

I thought we should make our way to my house. Daddy could hide Mr. Strong in the coal cellar until this thing blew over. But the editor wouldn't hear of it. He wouldn't endanger my family, he said. He wanted to make for Eagle Island or the swamps to the west of the city. He could hide for a couple of days, then jump a train heading north.

I peeped out from under the prickly leaves but saw no one about. We were just getting to our feet when I heard a carriage, and in a minute, it came barreling around the corner. Miss Morris was driving it. She was taking the corner on two wheels, leaning into the curve like a jockey at the race course.

"Hey, there!" I yelled. I jumped into her path.

"Whoa, whoa!" she called to her horse, and slowed enough for Mr. Strong to grab the bridle.

"Troy, why aren't you home with your family? There's a riot going on!"

"Miss Morris, this man needs your help."

"Aren't you Alex Strong?" she said. "You have to get away from here. I know of a place outside town where the train slows before it crosses the trestle bridge. I'll take you there, and you can leap aboard the 11:10. Please hide yourself under this blanket. You mustn't be seen."

"No," said Alex Strong.

I marveled at the two of them, so calm and polite. My eyes were beginning to burn. Smoke was filling up the sky, coloring it a horrible brown.

"I won't leave Wilmington hiding behind a woman's skirt," Mr. Strong continued. "I'll sit here, if you don't mind."

He climbed up beside her and took the reins from her hands.

"Troy," he said, "get in under this blanket. You mustn't be seen."

Mr. Strong geed up the horse as I knelt down at their feet and pulled the blanket over my head.

We'd gone about two miles when I felt the buggy slow.

"Sentries," muttered Mr. Strong.

We stopped abruptly, and the horse shied as if someone had grabbed her bridle. I could smell the stench of sulfur from a torch.

"Howdy, sir, ma'am. I'd like to know how come you're leaving town? Don't you know there's a necktie party going on in Wilmington?" It was the voice of a young boy.

"Is that so?" Mr. Strong said.

"Yes, indeed, we're lynching that *Courier*'s editor tonight. You've got to turn this buggy around and help us. Have you got a gun?"

"No, I'm afraid not."

"Here," the youthful voice said, "take mine."

"Hey, now, Tom, wait a minute," interrupted another voice, a voice that was nearly as familiar as my own. "You can't give him your gun. What'll you do if we catch the rascal? Bite him?" Randy said.

"That's all right, boys," Mr. Strong interrupted. "We can't stay for the lynching. We've got to get to New Bern tonight. My wife's sister—well, there's a lying-in, you see."

"Oh. Well, you get along, then. Good night, ma'am."

"Good night," said Miss Morris. And we drove on at a gallop.

I felt myself tossed about like a sack of potatoes, but I didn't care. I couldn't get the sound of Randy's voice out of my ears.

We'd gone a scant half mile when Miss Morris gave a shout.

"Look over there, Troy! Brooklyn's on fire!"

"Let me out!" I yelled. "I've got to find Momma and Callie."

The next thing I knew, I was standing in the middle of the street and the buggy was gone. It was a scene straight out of Momma's bible. I had gone to Hell.

THE
PELICANS

T HE SKY WAS AN UGLY COLOR, AND THE AIR WAS THICK WITH
  choking smoke. People in the streets were screaming, running every which way, like chickens after the
fox has got into the henhouse. Men on horseback rode
up and down, hooting, hitting people with their rifle
butts, and firing into the air. Dogs barked and bayed.
Above every other noise, a rooster was crowing, over
and over, as if day was about to break.

This was my street, where I had been born and
had grown up. I stumbled. But I kept moving. My
heart lifted when I saw my front porch. The house was
still there. I ran around to the back door.

It was locked!

I banged and knocked and made a baby of
myself, crying, "Momma, it's Troy, it's Troy! Let me in!"
But no one answered.

As if in a dream, I crossed the yard to the Hollis's oak tree. I shimmied up the trunk and laid myself down on the wide, sheltering limb. Hugging it with all my might, I closed my eyes.

I must have dozed for a few minutes or fainted, because when I lifted my heavy lids, there were some men underneath the tree.

"When's the governor's train arriving?" one asked.

"Ten o'clock on the Central Line."

A third man laughed. "Governor Russell is a mighty big man. Has anybody found a rope that'll hold him?"

"We could mosey on down to Zadoc's store, but I guess it's out of business by now."

That sounded like Mr. Hollis's voice.

"Where's Cantwell?" the first man asked.

"He said he was going to the depot to pay his respects—whether to the governor or his corpse, I don't know."

They all laughed. A gunshot sounded.

"Run for your lives, white men!" came another voice from down the street. "What liar told you that you can burn Big Isaac out of his home and live to see another morning on God's green earth?"

I squeezed my eyes shut in fear, praying that nothing bad would happen.

One of the men turned, lifted his rifle, and fired.

There came an answering shot, then, all at the same time, a blaze of rifle fire and a howl of pain and a woman's scream. One of the men below me collapsed into the dust. The other two knelt beside him.

"You there! Pinck!" a woman's voice cried. "You've killed Big Isaac! You and your Secret Nine!"

"Speak with respect, Peggy Ace, or my men will scorch the rest of your face. You'll wish you'd died before they get through with you," Capt'n Pinck hollered. "Throw aside that pistol, woman, or I'll shoot you down like I did that mad dog."

There was a volley of gunfire, and I saw Pinck's hat fly from his head, but he never flinched. He raised his rifle, took aim, and squeezed the trigger.

Silence but for the sounds I now was used to: sobs, crackling embers, distant gunshots. Pinck lowered his firearm. The other man whistled under his breath.

"Good shot. Now, help me drag Hollis here into his house."

"You drag him," Pinck said. "I'm going to the depot."

The wind picked up, and suddenly the air was bright with firebrands: slivers of burning wood rising into the air and flitting and glowing like ghosts.

When dawn broke, the skies began to drizzle. I was shivering. I climbed down from my perch as slowly and achingly as a rheumatic old man.

My street was scarcely recognizable. Half the houses were leveled, reduced to charred ruins. Someone had taken the bodies of Big Isaac and Peggy Ace and hanged them by the neck from a rafter. They turned slowly, this way and that. Mr. Hollis was lying on his porch, his feet turned out, his arms stretched above his head. I couldn't help but notice that his eyes were open, staring at the ashen sky. Then there was too much water in my eyes to see anything.

I walked slowly around to the back of my house and banged on the kitchen window.

"Momma?" I yelled.

"Troy?" It was Daddy's voice coming from the coal cellar. The trapdoor opened, and there he was, with Momma and Callie close behind. I was crying in earnest now, as much for them as for me. They couldn't know what was lying in the road outside, and I couldn't tell them.

Momma took me into her arms and began rocking me back and forth, humming under her breath. I wrapped my arms around her and held on.

Presently, there was a knock at the front door. Momma lifted her head and looked at Daddy. Callie began to cry quietly. She was holding her doll tight against her cheek. I pulled away from Momma and put my arm around her.

"Anyone home?" came a clear voice. "Mrs. Worth, it's me, Pamela Morris."

"Go, James," Momma said. My father squared his shoulders and walked into the next room.

"Did Troy get home last night, Mr. Worth?" Miss Morris asked before she was even in the door. "I've been so worried. We left him right in the middle of the conflagration, you see, and I'll never forgive myself if—" Then she saw us.

"What's going on out there, Miss Morris?" my mother asked.

The schoolteacher shook her head and wouldn't answer.

"You must gather your belongings and catch the first train out of town. The roads are clogged with people trying to leave. It's said the governor came in on the train last night, but never even got out of his carriage. The mob started beating in the windows and threatening to shoot the engineer. It was only after some of the governor's friends started firing shots into the crowd that the train was permitted to leave the station."

"Oh, my land," said Momma. She seemed curiously calm, almost as if she was hearing a story from long ago.

"Mr. French and Mr. Heeks have been arrested," Miss Morris continued. "They may be hanged by the vigilantes. Mrs. Heeks—well, nobody knows where she is. I've heard there are bodies floating in the Cape Fear River, and the killings may begin again soon. That Colonel Cantwell has made himself mayor, and Capt'n Pinck is chief of police. Lawyer Upton has disappeared, and his fine home was burned to the ground last night." She paused and shook her head sadly.

"Tomorrow was to have been voting day. I drove past the polling stations. There are armed guards outside keeping everyone away, Republican and Democrat. I just don't know what can be done!"

"But, Miss Morris, what happened last night?" I

broke in. "Did Mr. Strong get away?"

My parents looked from me to the schoolteacher with surprise.

"Yes, Troy, he got on the train, and God willing,

he is in Maryland by now. I told him to go to my family's home in Philadelphia. He is a brave man. I hope this doesn't break his spirit."

Miss Morris shook my momma's hand and Daddy's, and then kissed me and Callie on the cheek. She said she was going to the swamps to bring food to the scores of people hiding there. She didn't seem to have any fears for her life.

My mother was looking around her, as if she didn't recognize our home. She went to the parlor table and picked up the family bible.

"Let's go, James," she said. "I'm ready."

We joined a parade of sorry black folks trudging through the rainy streets. I saw Turps Etheridge plodding beside his wife, balancing a rolled-up feather bed on his head. Mrs. Etheridge was dragging a sack of their possessions.

Turps told my father that the bogs were full of terrified people but that he was going to get the train for Baltimore or Philadelphia or New York, as far away from Wilmington he could get.

"I just hope we can afford the tickets," he added.

The depot was packed with people, but Daddy found room for us in a cattle car. There we waited, shivering in the morning chill, for the train to leave. A child was whimpering. Her mother took up a hymn, and other voices chimed in: "When the battle's over we can wear a crown in the new Jerusalem."

I wanted the train to go. I looked into the faces of the armed men surrounding us. These people had been our neighbors. Now they were strangers. I wanted to do something, something to hurt them, to make them look me in the face and recognize me.

"Clear the way, clear the way!"

More Red Shirts rushed onto the platform. They were laughing and whooping, and they dragged a man at the end of a rope.

"Dear God, dear God," muttered my father. I looked closer and recognized the man to be Mr. Zadoc.

My mother put her hand on Daddy's arm, "Do you think they're going to hang him, James?" she whispered. "Can't we do anything?"

Colonel Cantwell had come to the front of the pack.

"My first act as the new mayor of Wilmington," he proclaimed triumphantly to all of us, "is to bid farewell to one of the carpetbaggers who so generously assisted the negroes of this town in their conspiracies. The Secret Nine who now govern this great city invite him to shake the dust of Wilmington from his feet. If he should return—and let this be a lesson to all assembled here—he'll find himself dangling from a strong tree limb."

The Red Shirts cheered, and Mr. Zadoc was hurled forward, tripping over the rope toward the train. My father leaned over and pulled him into our car.

The train heaved suddenly, built up a head of steam, and slowly pulled out of the station. There were cries from the people left on the platform. They ran alongside, trying desperately to throw their belongings on to the roof and hand their children to whoever would take them.

"I would like to spin a rope to hang each and every one of you," yelled Cantwell over the noise of the engine. "But I will be satisfied with seeing the sun set on such a rabble of ragtags! Go now, and don't stop until you reach Yankee-land."

"Good advice," muttered Mr. Zadoc. His eye was bruised, and there were rope burns around his neck and wrists, but he managed a half smile. "I recommend you follow it, Mr. Worth."

My father looked away so that no one could see him crying. A sob went up from a man crouched in the corner of the car.

"Upton, is that you?" asked Mr. Zadoc.

It was. His clothes were in tatters. His feet were bare and his face was stained with mud.

"It's all my fault," he cried wildly. "I never delivered the letter. I was too scared, too scared to go there at night. The Red Shirts—" he broke off and clenched his fists over his head.

"Don't carry on, Upton," Zadoc said matter-of-factly. "This was the plan all along, don't you see? It wouldn't have mattered what we did or didn't do. The Secret Nine wanted a riot and, by God, they made one. The city belongs to them now. And good riddance," he added, as he spat through the open door.

FROM THE TRAIN, I GLIMPSED THE SWELLS OF SAND ALONG the Cape Fear River. Silvery smooth tide pools glinted

through stands of long–leaf pine. Already the few scattered buildings on the city's edge were fading away in the distance. I felt like my heart would break seeing the last of home.

Momma leaned her head on Daddy's shoulder. Callie was beside me, staring straight ahead.

I followed her gaze. Off in the distance was a pelican roosting on an old fence post. When the train let out its long lonesome whistle, the brown bird turned its head to watch us go. Ever so sluggishly, it extended scrawny wings and began to flap its way into the sky, heading toward the water, toward Wilmington.

I pulled Callie over onto my lap.

"Look, honey," I said. "The pelican is saying

good-bye to us. People tell me that pelicans have the souls of Carolinians who died somewhere far off and weren't buried in their homeland. Someday we might come back to Wilmington as pelicans."

Callie turned her body around so that she could look me in the face.

"Speak for yourself, Troy Worth," she said. "I'm never coming back here."

I shook my head. She was right. We were never coming back. I glanced outside again. In the shallow ditch threading its way beside the train tracks, I noticed a boy hunched against the drizzle. He looked like he was waiting for somebody, searching the train's windows for someone in particular. As the engine slowed before crossing the trestle bridge, I was close enough to see that the boy was Randy.

His eyes fastened on my face, and he didn't stop looking as the cattle car pulled alongside, then passed him. But he said nary a word. Neither did I. Neither did my momma or my daddy or Callie.

After we'd crossed the bridge, I leaned out the door, and saw him still standing there, watching us go.

BIBLIOGRAPHY

Cashman, Diane Cobb. *Cape Fear Adventure*. Woodland Hills, California: Windsor Publications, 1982.

Chestnutt, Charles W. *The Marrow of Tradition*. Ann Arbor, M.I.: University of Michigan Press, 1969.

Dancy, John Campbell. *Sand Against the Wind*. Detroit: Wayne State University Press, 1966.

Edmonds, Helen G. *The Negro and Fusion Politics in North Carolina, 1894-1901*. Chapel Hill: University of North Carolina Press, 1951.

Evans, W. McKee. *Ballots and Fence Rails: Reconstruction on the Lower Cape Fear*. New York: Norton, 1974.

Hayden, Harry. *The Story of the Wilmington Rebellion*. [Wilmington, N. C.] c. 1936.

Prather, H. Leon, Sr. *Resurgent Politics and Educational Progressivism in the New South*. Cranberry, N.J.: Association of University Presses, 1979.

————— *We Have Taken a City: The Wilmington Racial Massacre and Coup of 1898*. Cranberry, N.J.: Association of University Presses, 1984.

Wrenn, Tony. *Wilmington, North Carolina: An Architectural and Historical Portrait*. Charlottesville, V.A.: University Press of Virginia, 1984.

AUTHOR'S NOTE

Although this novel is set in a real city during an actual event, the characters, their words, and their actions were either invented or else liberally blended from the actions and words of historical persons. The subject of the newspaper editor's editorial is factual, as are the results of the Secret Nine's conspiracy.

I am greatly indebted to *We Have Taken a City*, by H. Leon Prather, Sr., for its detailed descriptions of the riot and the events preceding it.